PRAISE FOR STEVE STRED

'Dark, gritty coming of age that grabs you near the end and doesn't let you go.'

Justin M. Woodward, Author of Tamer Animals about *The Girl Who Hid in the Trees*

'Brutal! Dark! Cults! Short! Novella! Twisted! Messed Up! Weird! Devils! Biblical! Ceremonies!'

Char from Char's Horror Corner about *Ritual*

'Ritual is a twisted, brutal novella that combines elements of extreme and subtle horror in a perfect blend.'

Jeremy Hepler, Bram Stoker Nominated Author of The Boulevard Monster about *Ritual*

'If you weren't scared of the woods after reading Steve Stred's excellent The Girl Who Hid in the Trees, then there's no doubt you will be after reading The Stranger.'

Morgan K. Tanner, Author of Army of Skin about *The Stranger*

'Wagon Buddy has a great ending and some awesome imagery. Though it's a simple story, it's a memorable one.'

J.H. Moncrieff, Author of Those Who Came Before about *Wagon Buddy*

'Yuri has the flavour of a dark, forgotten fairy tale from the frozen heart of Russia, and the writing is every bit as compelling as I've come to expect from Stred's stories.'

Christopher Henderson, Author of Artemis One-Zero-Five about *YURI*

'A grim, frost-bitten read, with a sense of icy hope at the core of its black, withered heart.'

David Sodergren, Author of The Forgotten Island about *Piece of Me*

'The One That Knows No Fear is a story that was literally dripping with nostalgia and horror in equal measure.'

Ross Jeffery, Author of Juniper about *The One That Knows No Fear*

'Ritual is a fast and thrilling dive into the depraved mind of a man and his dogma. It draws you into the horrors of a mysterious cult, and doesn't let go until the very last page. I loved this story.'

Sonora Taylor, Author of *Without Condition* and *Little Paranoias: Stories*

First published in Great Britain in 2020 by The Writing Collective.

ISBN: 978-1-7771571-4-2

1st Edition 2020

Cover Art by Mason McDonald

Copy Editing by David Sodergren

Formatting by Ross Jeffery

THE WINDOW IN THE GROUND

STEVE STRED

TWC

1

OH, I MUST HAVE BEEN FIFTEEN WHEN GRAMPS introduced me to the "*thing*" on the outskirts of town.

You see, back then folks treated it as a curiosity. A place to go and look, but not touch. My, oh my, you never touch. That was something that you needed to know. Never, ever touch.

A governance had been passed that no one under eighteen would be told about it, let alone see it. That's what the townspeople declared. Younger than eighteen are irresponsible and untrustworthy. Secrets need to be kept, they decided. Less chance of bad happening.

So, in the fifteenth year of existing – mind you back then, a fifteen year old was as much a child as a man - in mid-summer, I'm sitting in the shade outside, supposed to be mowing the lawn but not wanting to, when I see that big hunk of metal turn the corner near our house and pull into our driveway.

There was Gramps in his car and he yelled at me to get in.

'What's going on?' I asked.

'It's time', he answered. 'Your parents being too

chicken-shit to educate you so I'm gonna, otherwise I don't know what the hell's gonna happen. I ain't never gonna be responsible if things happen. Not me, no sirree.'

I was confused. But I went anyways. See, I trusted Gramps.

Where'd he take me?

Well, that's why you're here isn't it?

He took me to the window in the ground.

Things haven't been right since.

THE WINDOW IN THE GROUND RULES

No one under 18.
You must never be near it by yourself.
Minimum two people at all times.
Maintenance people must shield their eyes and plug their ears.
Absolutely no meat.
Under no circumstances will animals/pets be permitted.
No blood, this includes women during *that* time.
No babies.
Never, ever look in.
Never, ever touch it.
Failure to abide by these rules will result in swift and forceful punishment.
So it is decreed, on this day, by the power of the town council,

August 1st, 1674

2

No one's really sure how or why the window was put there, we just thank the good Lord above that it was. You see, that window protects us, keeps us safe, and more importantly, keeps us up here and whatever the hell that's down there, down there.

Gramps didn't say much on the drive. I sat quietly in the passenger seat, watching the trees go by. I saw my friend Fred playing hop-scotch outside his house. He must have swept the sidewalk off before laying down the chalk, because those white lines glistened. His leather shoes were all shined up as he tossed a rock then hopped to it. We didn't have much in the way of technology, not like folks now, but we made do with what we had and our imaginations. He looked as I went by and we both raised our hands sharing a sad wave. Part of me wondered if I'd ever see him again.

Gramps made a left at the end of the street, and I realized we were heading out of town. I hadn't left town in a few years. Wasn't much need to. We had everything here, even if outsiders looked at it like a shit-hole. We grew most of our produce in the back garden, and dad made a decent living at the mill. Mom baked and cooked like a professional chef, and with only my mouth to feed, I'd wager our family was more well off then a number of the others who had six or seven little ones running around. Heaven knows I'd heard people make comments about how lucky my parents were to only have one child while their gaggle ran amuck in the front yard.

Our little town had a campground on the outskirts, and I looked at the entrance as we drove by. I never paid much mind to it before, but as we passed, I saw dozens of folks parked in the parking area, checking in or out, I assumed. It struck me as odd that you'd want to camp there – there was no lake, the trees were rotting and for the life of me, I didn't believe there were even outhouses. Now, I couldn't be sure as I'd never spent much time there myself, but it looked like a place bodies get dumped.

It was at that moment that the smell of Gramps car hit me. You know what I mean – old man, tobacco smoke from his pipe and sweat. The material of the seats had never been cleaned or shampooed, so I started to picture all of the various butts that had sat on these seats, and just like that I was going to puke.

'Not in my car,' Gramps warned, somehow reading my mind, and pulled over.

I jumped out and dry-heaved for a few seconds before I stood and got back in. I cranked the handle and rolled the window down. Turning to see why Gramps hadn't started driving yet, I saw him sneering at me.

'What?' I asked, his look freaking me out.

'You got your daddy's gut', he said, before pulling

the lever down and we returned to the road, our mystery destination ahead. How far? I didn't know.

Looking back now, I should've recognized my stomach was trying to tell me to get away.

I didn't listen, and now I'm paying for that for the rest of my time on this godforsaken rock.

3

I MUST HAVE DOZED OFF AT SOME POINT, BECAUSE the next thing I heard was Gramps' door slamming shut, the hinges grinding and crying out for some TLC and his voice saying 'We're here, numb nuts.'

I rubbed my eyes and straightened up in the seat. Back then the cars didn't have seatbelts, so I opened my door and stepped out.

Gramps had driven us up some back road. In one direction I could look down the valley behind us and see the outline of the town. I also saw that the sun had moved across the sky. I wasn't an expert by no means, but looking at where it was now, I figured we'd been driving for a few hours.

The lot was deserted, but two logs had been placed at the edge some time ago. They'd been put purposefully with a gap between them. The gap was a start of a gravel path and I could see it head off into the woods, disappearing a few hundred yards ahead. The logs were a cheap, makeshift barricade, but also formed a nifty perimeter for any cars parking.

I felt all the skin on my body want to crawl off when I saw the dark opening ahead.

'Come on boy, we gotta get going,' Gramps called.

I hustled to catch up as he walked away.

No part of me wanted to follow, but every part of me wanted to know what was up that path.

4

WHEN THE PATH REACHED THE WOODS AND I followed Gramps in, well, that was the end of my youth and the beginning of being a man.

I didn't want any of this, nor did I ask for it. But I also went along by my own free will. Gramps didn't force me and never once did I say I wanted to turn around.

I don't care what you hear or what people say at the grocery store or playing cards on a Friday night.

I'm my own man and I made my own decisions, I tell you what.

I came awfully close though, to turning around, when we got to that signpost. I came even closer when we got to the clearing, but I didn't and here we are.

No one to blame but myself.

5

WE'D BEEN WALKING FOR CLOSE TO AN HOUR when the trees alongside the path closed in and I saw that they'd grown thick and tall. They were probably the oldest living things in the area, and a part of me wanted to stop and smell them – touch their bark and say thank you for existing. But I knew if I did that, I'd risk either getting smacked upside the head by Gramps or he'd just keep going and I'd be alone and lost in this unfamiliar place.

My admiration of the trees around us took my attention away and I ended up walking into the back of Gramps. He'd stopped in the middle of the path, and I just didn't see it. Thankfully he was more focused on the thing before him, and muttered for me to pay attention.

I stepped to his side and looked at what was before him and saw a sign post.

I read the rules, as you've done by now, and whistled loudly when I spotted the date.

'Keep it to yourself,' Gramps said. 'They weren't good men then, and they ain't worth nothing now.'

Then he told me to read the rules again and make sure I had 'em memorized.

'Is there going to be a test?' I sarcastically replied, smiling my goofy smile.

I was swatted across the side of the head hard and he told me to stuff it.

'Things like this will keep you alive,' he said and continued walking, leaving me to rub the spot where he'd hit me.

6

I FOLLOWED GRAMPS TOWARDS AN UNCERTAIN place, but I can tell you whole-heartedly, when I looked back and saw the signpost swallowed up by the path, I felt a lump grow in my throat and it was all I could do to not piss myself. Fear's a real feeling, if you didn't know. Fear'll make a man do cowardly things as well as heroic things, and I knew at that moment the coward in me wanted to flee.

You can think what you want about me,

But you weren't there,

And reading this don't make you no expert, that's for goddamned sure. I wish I could sit back with a smoke now, on this porch, my rocking chair creaking. But I can't and I know it would've done no damned good if I hadn't of followed. The same events would've played out, the same folks would've died, and I'd still be sitting, guilty as all sin.

Look – you know what you're getting into by reading this here account, by flipping these here pages. **People are gonna die and that's that**. I can't go back and change the past; I can't make folks walk and talk that are six feet under, or in some cases far deeper. No sir.

No sir.

But what I can do is tell folks what happened. I'm gonna die at some point here. Could be today, could be tomorrow, but at least if I get some of what went down off my chest, maybe I can meet my maker and he'll show some leniency. Whether I'm upstairs in the clouds or downstairs in the fire, I'll have told my truths and ain't no one can take that from me.

So, as I was saying, I followed Gramps and we trudged down that gravel path. You ever go hiking in the deep, dark woods? The places where most folks don't hike? If you have, you'll know what I mean. If not, take my word for it – but in the deepest, darkest places in the woods, the air's cold, the trees are mean and the animals are at the top of the food chain.

As we moved further along Gramps told me to watch the edges for any animals that might try to grab me, pull me into the forest.

'They pick off the smallest, the weakest,' he said, chuckling as he eyed my stature up, all five and a half feet of me and a hundred and twenty pounds.

I was trying to be brave and make him proud, but now it was like he was purposefully working to scare me, make me run.

Now when I think about it, he was testing me and I wished I'd failed.

7

THE TRAIL CONTINUED FOR SOME TIME, THE terrain flat and level. Then we both felt the path began to climb up the mountain.

Now, I'd never been a fan of the wilderness, I didn't like hiking, didn't like camping and preferred to stay indoors and read some mystery or western books.

My parents forced me to spend time outside, and my dad would compliment me on the most mundane task I'd complete, as though his ongoing praise would suddenly create a love of being out of the house.

'You mowed the lawn, what a champ,' he'd say, giving me a high five. Or, 'wow, thanks for walking to the store and back, way to go.'

His compliments, while appreciated, wouldn't change my mind. I hated the outdoors. If you like going outside, that's fine by me, enjoy your time with nature. Not this guy. Not now, not ever.

Hiking with Gramps up this ridiculous path, surrounded by murderous predators and weird bugs, was starting to really get me sour.

'How much longer?' I asked, sounding like a whiny toddler.

'Shut up and keep walking,' Gramps replied. The further along we went the worse his mood was. I didn't realize it then, but the closer we got to the reveal, the more anxious he became.

My legs were on fire and my lungs were burning as we kept climbing.

Soon I began to think my mind was playing games on me. A dozen more steps and I knew it wasn't; the ground was flattening. The gravel path straightened and then we came to a clearing.

The area was covered by pristine grass. Near the path entrance I saw an old rusty push mower propped against the base of the tree. Figures, I thought, ain't no one gonna haul that thing up and down to keep the grass mowed tight.

Near the back of the clearing, I saw the ground was *different*. I was too far away, too short to make out what it was but my blood ran cold when I saw the spot. That was why gramps had dragged my rear end up this mountain, through those woods. To show me whatever *that* was.

'Now listen here, boy,' Gramps said, his words cutting through the total silence of the day. I couldn't remember the last time I'd heard birds chirping or squirrels chattering. This was a place the earth didn't like, I could feel it through the stiff soles of my oxfords, could taste it on my tongue, smell it in my nose with each breath.

Gramps continued, ignoring my distracted gaze.

'You read the sign, you remember the rules? We're gonna walk over there,' he said pointing at the disturbance in the ground.

'It's gonna make you feel weird and make your insides wobble and that little pecker in your pants throb, that's all part of its game, its con. Keep your wits about you, boy. The rule said – never be near by yourself. So's I see you do something *off*, I'm gonna act accordingly. Same for you to me. I start acting puffy or whatever, you tackle me down and smack me 'til I return, got it?'

I nodded as though I was on board, but I still had no clue.

I followed my beloved Gramps 'cross that clearing.

Followed him to his grave.

8

WE SLOWED THE CLOSER WE GOT, AND EVEN though the grass looked the same, it became crunchier nearer the mound. As though the ground was harder, drier, sucking the essence from the earth.

'Gramps, can we go back?' I asked. I sounded scared, but I didn't care. I'm a coward, I'll admit it. Some of what happens later might make you change your mind, but rest assured, I'm no hero.

'Shut your mouth you panty-waist,' he replied, his voice wavering as well. 'We came this far, I ain't letting you skip out on this. You need to know.'

As we made our final few steps, I saw that around the mound was a path made of gravel. It was edged by larger, thicker rocks. Someone did a thorough job of maintaining this place, I thought.

'Here we are, boy. We don't know how, or why, or when, but here we are. This is our town's secret, our town's shame, but for many of us, the pride of our town. It makes us unique, you see. No one else has one, as far as we know. We've hired fortune tellers, ghost talkers, even went and talked to some priests.

They all struck out or thought we were nuts. Well, who's nuts now? See, boy. This here, is *ours*.'

I stepped around Gramps to see what he was motioning at and felt my knees grow weak and my stomach lurch. I couldn't breath and the sky swam with red and orange flames.

'You feel it, eh? It'll do that to you. This here is what you need to see now. This here is the window in the ground. May the good Lord above continue to keep it closed.'

9

I CAN'T TELL YOU HOW LONG I STOOD IN SILENCE beside Gramps. I wish I could, but time paused and I stared blankly at the spectacle before me.

There, *right there*, in front of my young eyes was a raised mound of cement and in the middle was a window.

A goddamned window.

I'm no good with estimates, but I'd peg it to be close to ten feet long and five feet wide. It was shaped a bit like an egg and I could see there were cross beams from my position. I took a tentative step closer, but Gramps' arm shot out and his hand pressed on my chest, preventing me from approaching.

'Careful,' he said quietly.

'I just want to take a closer look,' I replied.

'Remember the rules,' he said gruffly.

I heard a noise and looked at the trees beyond the clearing, seeing the leaves and branches blow around in the wind higher up. Even though I couldn't feel any wind I found myself getting colder under the mid-afternoon sun.

Woof.

A sound like a dog barking or a flame igniting came from within, or underneath the window, to be more accurate. Then I heard shuffling and scraping and I turned to run, but again Gramps held me tight. Someone or something was down there. My eyes were wide with fear and as Gramps held me close, I started to cry.

'I'm sorry, son,' he said, as he hugged me tight. 'You needed to know. It's a lot, but crying's ok. I ain't gonna judge you on this one, boy.'

As he rocked me, squeezing my shoulders and back like only our grandparents can, a scream pierced through the window, followed by the scratching of claws longing to escape.

I screamed.

He didn't hit me, didn't swear, didn't even step back and tell me to shut up. He just hummed a tune while holding me close while the window fought to stay shut.

10

Once I finally calmed down, the tears stopping, Gramps released me and stepped back.

I was so ashamed, but when I looked at Gramps, I knew he wasn't judging me. He gave me a look that said he was proud I hadn't fought his embrace and ran back down the hill.

'Now,' he said, 'you'll have questions. I won't be able to answer most of 'em, but let's have a seat and I'll do my best.' I was about to protest sitting on the grass near the window when I saw him walk towards a bench near the edge of the woods.

'Someone put a bench out here?' I asked.

'Sure,' Gramps said, 'there's a few of us who'll come out here and just sit and think sometimes. I'll come up here with my friend Bill and we'll shoot the shit or just sit in silence and listen to what's going on down there. This bench has been here longer than I've been alive.'

We sat on the bench and I found that from our position I could make out light coming from the window. The light also showed me that the window had a thick buildup of grime on its surface.

'That a candle down there? Or a lantern?'

'Not sure,' Gramps answered. 'I've certainly never looked into the window. Don't believe no one's gone down and lived to come back up.'

'If we don't know anything about it, why does the town take care of it?'

'Ahh, now that's a smart question,' Gramps said, wide grin painting his square jaw.

I felt a flush course through me, glad to have made Gramps happy, even here, at *this* place.

'You see, son, the town cares because we fear this place so, so much. Our fear runs through us like it's one with our blood. We need to make sure this place is ok. And maybe, if it is the gateway to somewhere else, whoever is in charge there will look upon us with favor, for tending to the grass and keeping the area clean.'

'Makes sense,' I said, as I stood and stretched. I looked at the window and I felt Gramps stand beside me. He wasn't taking any chances.

'So, *no one's* ever looked in there?' I was dumbfounded that not one person had ever looked before, and I could tell the question ruffled Gramps.

'Boy, no one's ever looked in that's lived. Sure, some folks have looked in there, but no one's alive that can tell you what's down there.'

He paused then, looking around, as though worried he'd be caught with his hand in a cookie jar.

'There's been a few folks over the years that tried to look in on their own, but it didn't end well for any of 'em. Wilf Russell's body was found on the trail some years back. He was heading back to town. When he was found his eyes had burst inside his head and his tongue was all swelled up like he'd stuck it in an angry hornet's nest. He had a piece of paper in his pocket and he'd sketched something on it. When the mayor and constable found out what he'd sketched on that piece of paper, well... we never saw the folks again who found Wilf or who looked at that paper.'

Another pause. Another series of darting glances.

'As far as I know, the paper was lit on fire and destroyed.'

'Oh,' I meekly replied. My curiosity was growing the more Gramps spoke. I was young then, didn't know better.

'Then there was Sven Thordssen. He moved here to start a new life and it didn't last long. No one'll admit to bringing him up here, but he was found here nonetheless.

They found his body right close to where we're standing. He'd scratched his eyes out and dug into his ears so hard that brain matter was found under his nails. When the doc cut him open his stomach was full of blood and they said it was from screaming so loud that his throat burst and he swallowed it all before dying. Doesn't sound like a fun way to go, does it?'

Gramps chuckled then, as he looked off into the distance and absently pawed at his pipe that wasn't there.

'There's only been one *incident* in my lifetime, at least that I'm aware of. I don't get any special privileges or nothing, but we all heard about what happened to Douglas McCarther some years back. I was thirty the year it happened.'

As Gramps said the man's name a ghastly roar bellowed from below and something immense bashed against the ground beneath us. I steeled my nerves, struggling to not run. I expected a grotesque hand to shoot up and pull our bodies below, to whatever fate met those down there.

Gramps waited for it to subside, then continued.

'From the tales told, the town council at the time was up here having a meeting about an amendment to one of those rules listed. Douglas was known to be a calm, rational man, but at the meeting he was yelling, swearing and becoming erratic. He began to push some of the men, screaming that it was time for everyone to learn the truth. He then rushed to the edge of the window and began to grab at it, as though he was going to open it. The last thing he said was 'no, no, no, it can't be!''

Gramps fell silent then, looking at the ground, absently kicking the gravel with the end of his shoe.

'What happened, grandpa? Did he open the window? Fall in?'

Gramps looked me in the eyes then, and I didn't like what I saw.

'The constable shot him in the back of the head. He died right over here,' Gramps said, walking to the other side of the mound. Squatting down I could see a tiny square piece of wood with the initials DM carved into it.

'They don't want folks up here leaving flowers or nothing, so they told everyone he had a heart attack on the walk down and they buried his body in the cemetery. But this is where he was killed. Truth be told he died the second he tried to open that window.'

As we stood then, quietly looking at the little wooden remembrance piece, a noise came from the window. It sounded like a long fingernail being pulled across the surface of the glass.

The noise had a purpose, I knew. It was trying to get me to look.

I wanted to so badly.

11

After some time, Gramps made a motion letting me know it was time to go.

'Gotta get back before dark,' he mumbled, 'don't want your parents to know what I've done.'

I was trembling. I didn't know how to process just what I'd been exposed to. There was A. WINDOW. IN. THE. GROUND. There were *things* below it. As we left, the sun was beginning to set on the day, the light growing orange and lush. When we made it to the end of the clearing, I looked back. I was young then, innocent and curious, you see, I wanted to know what was down there. Standing there, I knew I'd been better off having let Gramps go on his own. I would've mowed the lawn gladly instead.

It had grown dusk enough that I could very well make out the yellow light shining from within. I saw some shadows writhing. Gramps put his hand on my shoulder, making me jump.

'Sorry, boy,' he softly said. 'Sorry, for what I've done to ya.'

I nodded and we walked away, descending down

the gravel path. At first it was flat again, then began to slope off steadily.

It was just me and him then. I felt some tears come, trickle down my cheek and Gramps kept his old leather mitt of a hand on my shoulder, squeezing in comfort. When I snorted to clear my nose and try to stem the tide of waterworks, he stopped and we stared at the foreboding forest before us.

'I've made you a man today, far earlier than you'd expected. For that, I'm sorry. But you gotta believe me when I tell ya, it was for your own good, boy. I wouldn't want ya to stumble on this, discover what's up here and stand twiddling my thumbs while you get executed. Love you too much to let that happen.'

He left me standing there, absorbing what he'd said.

From behind me came the cackling of some unknown thing, forcing me to run to catch up.

12

WE HIKED DOWN IN SILENCE.

We paused for a moment when we arrived at the sign post. I re-read the rules, burned them into memory. Wasn't something I'd ever forget, mind you, but I wanted to be sure.

It was full dark when we made it back to the car. When we got in, he took his time packing his pipe. The snap of the match igniting reminded me just how jittery I was.

After he'd taken a few puffs, he passed it my way. I'd never tried it before, never smoked a cigarette or had a beer, but things felt different. I put the pipe into my mouth, gave a few sucks, then coughed my lungs out. Normally I'd have expected Gramps to laugh or give me a good tongue lashing about learning to be a man, but he just took the pipe back and then started the car.

We pulled out in silence.

How I'd sleep tonight, I didn't know.

How I'd ever sleep again, I didn't know.

13

When we got home my parents ran to me, worried that something had happened. Gramps apologized but refused to tell them just where we'd been, what we'd been up-to.

'Made your boy a man,' he said, framing it as a joke. My parents didn't know the horrible truth of the statement though.

'Oh, dad, you didn't take him to Marge over on 3rd street, did you?' My dad tried to be quiet, but I heard. I wished Gramps had taken me to a prostitute. I'd have rather ended up needing penicillin for a month from that lonely old woman, than what we'd really been up to. Even having a case of a rash and itchy balls would have been preferred.

'No, I did not. Sometimes a man's gotta teach a youngin' how the world is,' Gramps replied. He patted my shoulder and gave my chin a pinch as he shuffled back into the car and left. I realized we would've made better time if Gramps hadn't had such bad hips and knees. But the life he lived wouldn't let him have it any other way.

'You hungry?' Mom asked. I was famished and

devoured the potatoes, squash and pork chops that she'd made. It was getting pretty late, that night, and even though it was summer and I didn't have school the next day, my dad said maybe I'd better head upstairs and get ready for bed.

Bed. Sleep.

The thing I wished I'd never have to face was coming soon.

Just what would the night bring me?

14

FUNNY, THE WAY OUR BRAINS WORK. SOME events happen and they stick with you, until your dying days. Other things come along and you forget 'em an hour later. You've all experienced it; another driver doesn't see you and you almost get side-swiped. Most people'll have forgot about it by dinner time.

You'd think I would've had nightmares every night for the rest of life.

Thing is, I didn't have nightmares that night. I didn't start having dreams about that there window in the ground until this last year. Maybe my brain finally up and decided to start punishing me for all I seen, all I witnessed. Maybe it was my punishment for not doing more, not stopping what was started that day that Gramps took me up.

Who's to say? Not me, that's for damn sure. Not me.

15

I WOKE UP THE NEXT MORNING WITH A headache. My eyeballs hurt in my head and my neck was stiff like I'd slept with it tilted way back.

By the time I made my way downstairs, dad was long gone to work and mom must've went to visit some friends. I found some cold eggs and hard toast on the table with a note beside it.

It was just a quick little squiggle of a heart, which I knew my mom had left behind. She'd made an effort, so I wasn't about to hold that against her. Wasn't her fault her son slept in.

I ate the eggs and slathered the hard bread with lots of jam and finished it up quick. The cold glass of milk I got from the fridge was icing on my cake. It cut through the ashy texture of the bread.

I knew dad still expected me to mow the lawn, but I just couldn't bring myself to do it. I wasn't the same boy I was yesterday. I was a man now, heck I'd smoked a pipe. Now I had this godforsaken stake being driven into my head and I knew it was from whatever it was down *there*.

Now, I think I've established that I ain't the

smartest of people. No, I've got some redeeming qualities, mom always said it was a good thing I had dimples when I smiled, so what I did next isn't something I'm proud of, nor is it something that had me use my brains.

I finished eating, put the dishes in the sink then walked outside. I walked straight over to my friend Fred's place. Not seeing him out front, I knocked on the screen door.

When his mom came to see who was banging so loudly, I almost lost my nerve. But then something squeezed me from the inside and I stammered it out.

'Is Fred home?'

His mom went and retrieved Fred who looked startled to see me standing there.

We walked casually away from the house, over the hop scotch lines and then headed towards the park.

We got to the park and went and sat at a picnic table before either of us finally spoke.

'You look old,' Fred said.

'I'm a man now,' I replied, nothing but seriousness in my reply.

We sat in silence for another few minutes. I was relieved to hear the birds chirping. The sound was calming and helped me relax.

'My Gramps showed me something yesterday. Something... unbelievable,' I calmly said, measuring each word with the expression on Fred's face.

He nodded, and I wondered if he'd already been shown.

'You wanna go see it?' I asked.

'What is it?' He replied. I saw that even though the day was overcast and the air was cooler, Fred was sweating. His forehead could have used a dab with a handkerchief but I didn't have one and I suspected neither did Fred.

'It's a window. In the ground.' I expected him to burst out laughing or to nod like he'd already known, but instead his eyes went wide and I could tell he had no idea that it existed.

'We can make it if we leave now and take that rusty truck out by the hall,' I said. Part of me hoped Fred said no way, no chance, but instead he smiled and nodded and jumped up from the table.

'Let's go,' he said excitedly.

So I found myself walking with Fred, heading back towards that hole in the ground. I knew I shouldn't've been going, but damn if something wasn't leading me, forcing me.

Too late to say now.

Too late for a lot of things.

16

As I predicted, me and Fred made faster time than me and Gramps did. I knew something was guiding me because I didn't know how Gramps had got there. I had dozed off and slept while he drove. But not long after the campground I saw a trail leading into the woods, just off the road. We took the turn and ended up where Gramps had parked.

The gravel pathway and entrance into the woods leered at me, the opening to the *beyond* felt sinister and my stomach clenched.

I remembered how much the hike up had scared me, tired me and made me uncomfortable the further we'd travelled.

Now with Fred we laughed and joked as we walked. It was a very different experience with Fred than Gramps, but that's how it should be, right? Better with a friend than a family member?

When we arrived at the sign post with the rules I heard Fred exhale audibly, and watched as he read the rules.

'We ain't 18 yet,' he said.

'I know, but Gramps showed me yesterday, says better to know now.'

Fred shrugged and started walking away.

'Hold up, Fred. You read them? Memorize them. Gramps said it'd save my life, so the same to you. Read 'em, memorize them.'

Fred did a pirouette on one foot and trudged back over. I could tell he was getting annoyed already, but I knew that'd go away once he saw the mound.

'Got 'em,' he said, tapping his temple for posterity.

'Ok. The woods get... weird up here,' I said and we started again.

I saw Fred shiver when we entered the darker part of the path.

'Don't worry, the clearing's coming up after the hill,' I assured him.

Then the ground changed and we went up the hill.

I felt giddy with excitement, knowing the window was getting so close. My pulse quickened and I had to work to make sure I didn't break into a full run.

When we made it to the flat part again, I started to walk faster and Fred joined me, keeping pace. He felt it too, I looked at him and his eyes showed his eagerness.

What greeted us when we made it to the clearing wasn't anything we'd ever expected.

17

Back then things ain't like they are now.

We didn't have no internet or phones in our pockets.

Back then we didn't even really have magazines with naked ladies.

We had the Sears and Roebuck catalog and the women were drawn real scantily, but at 15 years old, I hadn't seen no naked women yet in my life. Not even an accidental glimpse of my mom.

As we approached the clearing we could hear chanting, people singing, and moans and groans.

Gramps had told me to tell him if I felt my Johnny Knobbler stirring when we were there yesterday, but it'd never even twitched.

Now hearing the noises I felt my crotch start to respond and by the way Fred started tugging at his trousers I knew he was in the same boat.

When we arrived at the clearing, well, there was more flesh than I'd ever know what to do with.

At least a dozen people were dancing around naked, a fire burning in the middle of them.

'Witches,' Fred gasped and I saw him look to run.

'Stay,' I said and grabbed his arm. We crouched down by one of the trees near the entrance.

I started to notice that the women dancing around were moving closer and closer to us. Did they know we were there? If they were witches then they should, yeah?

They danced near us and before we knew what was happening a lady with long brown hair and a smile that made me giggle grabbed my hand and led us out to join them. I looked over at Fred and his face was pure euphoria. A redheaded woman with more freckles than not was holding his hand and I could almost feel the heat she radiated through my friend.

Somehow we were disrobed, but we never stopped dancing, never stopped singing and smiling.

I found the grass below my feet soft and welcoming, which was odd because yesterday the stuff seemed brittle and that every step crushed and broke the stalks.

But now, under the grey clouds and the watching trees the grass felt like it was pulling me tighter to the ground.

18

I WOKE UP AS THE SUN WAS SETTING.

I heard Fred groan near me and I bolted upright. We'd been at the clearing with the window, the ladies had been dancing, and there'd been a fire.

I found I was fully clothed again, as was Fred.

I whirled around to find we were alone, just the two of us. No sign of a fire nor any hint of any dancing ladies.

'What happened?' Fred asked, standing and looking woozy.

'The ladies are gone,' I said. 'They must have charmed us or something?' I just didn't understand what'd happened. We'd been dancing and now we woke up alone. My brain just wouldn't compute.

'Thanks,' Fred said. I saw he had a grin on his face and his hair was matted and messed up. He plucked a comb from his breast pocket and licking it, he fixed his hair, made sure it puffed over and rolled, just like he liked it.

'For what?'

'You brought me here to see those ladies, didn't you?'

I pointed past him, pointed at the mound. He turned and even from behind I could see that his jaw dropped.

'What... is... that?'

He stammered it out and I knew that he hadn't noticed it when we'd been dancing with the mysterious women.

'That's the window in the ground,' I replied. 'That's what those rules are all about.'

'The... window... in...'

Fred's voice trailed off as he started to walk quickly towards the mound.

'Fred? Hold up, Fred. You can't look down there!'

I was practically shouting at him now as I ran, trying to get to him.

I saw I wasn't going to reach him in time, wasn't going to stop him from looking.

Just as Fred made it to the edge of the mound a crack echoed through the air and I dropped.

I knew it was a gunshot, the sound sending me to the gravel.

Fred was standing still, not moving. I didn't see no blood or nothing, so he hadn't been shot. I wasn't in pain, so I hadn't been shot. I guess the person fired a warning shot to stop Fred from doing something stupid.

I turned my head to see who it was and knew I was in a horse cart full of shit.

At the edge of the clearing was my dad, my gramps, Fred's dad and the constable.

Fred went pale white when he turned and saw who it was, surprising us all by not passing out.

'Boys, how 'bout you mosey your asses on over here,' the constable said. His voice had a deep timbre, one that vibrated throughout your conscience, letting you know you were in trouble.

I wanted to look casual, well as casual as I could, so I took my time and walked over calmly. My dad wouldn't make eye contact with me, but his face sure was red, hands clenched tight.

Gramps lips were pulled back in a sneer and if he could've beat me then and there he would've.

'Boys,' the big lawman said, 'what we have here is an 'incident,'' he said, making air quotes when he spoke incident. I gulped, knowing I'd never be leaving my room. At least I'd seen some naked ladies, I thought, because I'd never see one again.

'Usually, an incident like this would result in one of two things,' the constable said. I knew those two things wouldn't be good.

'Now, you may think I'm trying to scare you boys, and while I am, what I'm about to say are the agreed upon two options. Option one is that I shoot you both square in your forehead. Right between your fucking eyes. This here pistol will explode the back of your heads fair and true and you won't even feel a thing. You can even choose who goes first. Option two would be that we'd throw you down in that pit there. We'd walk over, use the metal pole we have there, open that window and then toss you in, game over. What's it gonna be?'

Both Fred and I pissed ourselves. I looked at him, he looked at me as the fronts of our trousers darkened. I stammered, I gagged, I struggled for breath. Then my dad was on me, holding me, helping me swim above this panic attack.

Fred's dad was with him as well, helping him to calm.

My dad spoke then and I was glad his voice was even and fair.

'We ain't gonna kill you boys. But consider this a hard lesson learned. Your Gramps shouldn't have brought you up here,' he said, before looking at Gramps. The old man turned his head away, eyes closing in shame.

'But, I'm glad he did. Still, you shouldn't have brought poor Fred up here. He didn't deserve to have nothing happen to him. If we hadn't got here in time who knows what could've happened.'

'Did the ladies tell you?' I asked.

The men all looked between themselves, confusion written across the creases in their brows.

'Ladies?' The constable's voice had somehow deepened in that one word.

'We came up here, because your mom was worried you'd been gone so long. When Gramps heard that Fred was with you, he had an inkling where you'd be heading. Here we are. Who were those ladies?'

I looked at Fred. I didn't know how much I was supposed to say.

Then he spoke up.

'When we got here, there were a bunch of naked ladies dancing around a fire and singing. They grabbed us and had us join in. They did something to us, we blacked out. We woke up, they were gone. Then you arrived.'

The adults all looked concerned.

'You boys head home now,' the constable said. 'Us adults have some things to discuss.'

Me and Fred didn't say nothing else. We ran the entire way down, and got home as fast as we could.

It wasn't until way later that night that I heard my dad return home.

19

I SHOULD'VE STAYED IN MY ROOM, LET HIM HAVE some time to cool down. But like I said earlier, I ain't all that smart and no amount of dimples was gonna calm him.

'Dad?'

I was standing at the entrance to the kitchen. Usually he didn't drink too much during the week, what with work and all, but I see him sitting at the table with two empty bottles laid on their sides and he was already working on a third. He looked over at me with eyes that hurt. I wished I was still in my room then. He looked disappointed, with a fire blazing just behind that emotion.

'Your Gramps is fucking lucky,' he said and I cowered. I'd never heard my dad swear before. Heck, Gramps himself barely swore.

'You and Fred are lucky to be alive,' he continued, taking a swig. I saw him set that cup down, his hand vibrating and causing it to clink and rattle on the wood top.

I wanted to change the subject, try to sound grown up, but I knew when I asked my next question, his expression told me I was treading on awful thin ground.

'Who were those women?'

The air in the room went from static electricity to funeral parlor from only four words.

My dad set the bottle down, turning in the chair to face me. Doing so dropped his face into the shadows, making me step back. It was as though he'd transformed from my parent to a blood-thirsty predator, ready to lunge.

'Your Gramps introduced you to a place you're not ready for. But I'm going to level with you, ok son? There are too many unknowns about that place. We don't know *what's* down there. We don't know *who's* down there. What we do know is that different groups, different people have their own beliefs as to just what's down there. Those women are one such group. They want to open the window and let out whatever it is down there. So, we stop them, keep that window shut.'

He turned then, his face rejoining the light, the predator disappearing and my lungs working again. He took a drink and I thought about what he'd said. I had questions, but for once I kept my trap shut. He still looked on edge and I didn't want to end up on the wrong side of those fists. My dad had never hit me before, but I'd never pushed him this far. Best to know my place and keep it.

I turned to leave and he cleared his throat, stopping me in my tracks.

'You ever go there again, I'll throw you in myself.' His voice was cold and it had the desired effect on my young mind. I hurried to my room when I heard him start to gulp more beer down.

20

I LAID LOW FOR A FEW DAYS, KEPT MY interactions with my parents to a minimum. I made sure I said my please and thanks, did my dishes without being asked.

I mowed the lawn. I picked some vegetables from the garden for mom and took the time to water everything.

But every single second of every single day was a struggle.

Something was boiling in me, I tell you.

It hurt and it needed to be released.

I would try and scratch, I would try and drink water fast, hoping a big belch would help, but nothing worked.

On the third day I asked if I may walk over and see Fred.

My mom said I could, but I needed to stay at his house and wrote a note to Fred's mom, telling her just that.

I rushed over to Fred's, excited to see my friend, even if it was under lock and key.

His mom didn't look too thrilled when I knocked on the door, but she read the note, let me in, and said Fred was in his room.

When I entered his room, I knew instantly that Fred had been dealing with the same issues.

21

'Fred, you doing ok?'

He was sitting there on his bed, looking like he'd made a halfhearted attempt to get ready that morning. He had his pants on, but they were still undone. One boot was on but not tied up, his other foot didn't have a sock yet.

He had no shirt on and I was shocked at what I was looking at.

I'd spent plenty of time with Fred at the swimming hole. It was a small little spot on the other side of town, only the locals knew about it. I'd seen Fred numerous times without a shirt. Sure he was thin and white as a sheet, but what I was looking at now wasn't Fred.

He'd lost an ungodly amount of weight since I'd seen him last, only a few days back, his bones poking out like he was part porcupine.

He had bright red marks all over his body, like someone had taken a crayon and used it to lash him with. I wanted to reach out and touch 'em, but the amount Fred was sweating kept my hands back.

'Those hurt?'

I asked it quietly, feeling little and inconsequential now.

'WHAT DO YOU THINK?' Fred yelled in reply, and I saw his skin pulse and push away from his body.

I took another step back, banging into the wall behind me. Defensively, my hands were raised and I looked for an exit. The door'd disappeared somehow, just four walls and Fred. I saw the bed starting to slither and writhe as though possessed.

'Fred? Fred?'

I spoke feebly as he stood and walked towards me. I shrank to the floor, bringing my legs in close, tucking my head between my knees.

'This is all your fault,' he said over and over.

Then I felt his burning hot hands digging into my neck and what I did next would've had Gramps in a fit of rage.

I screamed.

Jesus Christ.

I shouldn't go on no more.

I wanna just sit here and let my body go. I'd close my eyes, let the darkness descend and take my sins with me.

WHY DID I GO BACK?

You tell me! Why?

I shoulda known better! GODDAMN IT. I SHOULDA!

No. No.

Gramps should have never taken me.

Fucking old man. No, I don't mean that. I hope he is resting in peace.

Sorry.

I'm rambling.

OK.

I screamed.

22

I was still screaming when Fred's mom burst into the room. Fred was sitting on the bed now, but breathing in and out real hard, like he'd been running.

'Everything alright in here, boys?' she asked casually, as though it was totally normal for someone to be screaming for their life in her son's róom.

I didn't answer, I just got up to leave and as I got by her and into the hallway, Fred yelled after me.

'They'll be coming for you!'

I ran then.

I ran crying. I ran so hard my knees hurt.

I ran.

And then it was dark.

I found myself standing in front of the rules. The sign.

Somehow, I'd ended up at the sign and I knew my legs were gonna keep moving me towards that clearing, that mound and surely that window.

For something was boiling below the surface. Something wanting to burst forth.

I may not have the IQ of a genius, but I'm bright enough to know what was to come.

23

YOU EVER DRIVE SOMEWHERE, THEN THINK BACK and realize you don't remember parts of the drive?

Like a bridge or a town or a turn. Suddenly you're miles past it and your brain sends a message to you that somehow along the way you tuned it out?

Did I already say this? Did I? I'm too buggered to look back and see if I did, but if I did, just know it's because my mind's going.

Anyways, that was me that night, finding himself at the sign with the rules, then at the clearing. Standing at the entrance on the far side, I could see the mound.

I didn't have a watch, but it was now dark and lately it'd been getting dark around nine, so I knew it was pretty late. I also felt my guts clench and my palms get sweaty when I realized I was by myself, at night and under eighteen. I was breaking three rules in one sweeping motion and I was pretty sure I was gonna puke.

Then a scrapping and a clanging noise.

I looked at the mound and could see that a light

was shining up from the under, from inside the window. Something was happening below.

A new sound happened and I whirled around. This was coming from down the gravel path and was getting closer.

I ran to the trees lining the clearing, ran for my goddamned life.

I'd just jumped into the underbrush near the edge of the path when the noise arrived.

The moon was out and shining bright, but whatever the things were, I wasn't meant to see 'em.

A parade of chained creatures marched by, led by something stinking of garbage and rot. I could hear them panting and huffing, and I suspected the chains prevented them from walking with any sort of normality. I counted as they went by and there were eight chained beasts clanking along.

I waited for a thirty count, then slowly moved from my hiding place and crept to the edge of the clearing. I was just in time to see the last of the things jump down into the opening, the window now open and standing straight on edge. Once the last one was gone and down, the window slammed shut and I heard a latch clink into place.

I knew I should've left then, returned home. My mom and dad were probably frantic.

But I stayed.

I walked over to the bench, sat down and stared at the window in the ground, wishing that I could get the courage to go look down into the light.

24

'JUST WHAT IN THE HELL ARE YOU DOING?'

My dad's voice cut through the crisp dew of the morning and I came about, realizing I wasn't lying in bed. No, I was sitting on the bench in the clearing and I wasn't getting out of this one easy.

I stiffly stood, my body complaining about the hardness I'd slept on and I twisted and cracked my way to some semblance of feeling awake enough to walk over to him. I figured if I warmed up a bit now - if I had to run - I'd be ready.

I sheepishly walked over, tail tucked between my legs like a dog caught eating some shoes, and crossed the clearing.

'Dad...' I started, wanting to try and explain a bit, maybe make a dent in his fury, but it wasn't to be.

His right arm shot out and the short jab caught me right in the mouth and I dropped, seeing stars. I'd never been punched before in my life. I was surprised and hurt. From behind me, I could've sworn I heard chuckling from the window.

Now, here's a universal truth. Your dad, no matter how old he is, can kick your ass. Smirk, guffaw, bark at me, whatever you want. But it's the Lord's honest truth. And why's it possible?

Old man strength.

Men who work with their hands for a living have old man strength, and you can take that to the bank. Go to the gym for hours, do what you think you need to do, but at the end of the day, old man strength will kick your ass every time.

I experienced old man strength straight to my face and I was paying for it.

I rolled on the ground and held my jaw, but my dad wasn't having none of it. He started kicking me in my sides, my stomach and my back. He was shouting at me, swearing at me and I knew if the other person hadn't have grabbed him and told him that was enough, we'd probably still be there, only I'd be a bloody lump of ground beef.

'Enough on the kid.'

I'd never been so relieved to hear Gramps' voice. I should've suspected he'd be with dad, but I also didn't think I was gonna be spending the night where I did.

Gramps extended his hand and I accepted, letting him help me up. When I was standing, he gave me a good smack to the side of the face.

'You gotta learn, ya dipshit,' he said, and then hugged me, engulfed me in his arms and then my dad was wrapped around us as well.

We broke the hug after a few moments and I saw Gramps and dad were both wiping tears from their eyes. My dad touched my busted, swollen lip and softly apologized. I nodded. I knew. He had been worried. Worried that I'd been lost to them.

We walked away from the clearing, even with the

vibrations from some subterranean search calling through our feet.

We didn't speak a word until we arrived at Gramps' car. I was starving when we got in, but I sat silently, fearing a single spoken word would open up the dam, letting the feelings they had bottled up explode forth with more fury.

When we pulled up at the house, my dad got out, flipped the seat down, letting me emerge from the small back seat.

Gramps pulled away, leaving the two of us standing alone on the sidewalk, birds chirping. For most folks the day was beginning. Life was ready to greet them and introduce new challenges, new excitements, and old habits.

'Glad you're ok,' dad said, squeezing my shoulder.

'I saw something,' I said as he started walking. 'The window was open and something went in.'

My dad whipped around as though he was on some harness like they use in the movies nowadays.

'What did you say?'

'I saw something, well actually somethings, and they went into the window. It was open.'

My dad's mouth dropped open and he looked frantically around. I wasn't sure if he was ensuring no one heard me or wanted to find someone else to tell the news to.

Instead he grabbed me by the arm and hauled me inside.

Then I sat at the kitchen table waiting.

Waiting for my dad to return with the mayor, the constable and the other town councilmen.

25

I MUST HAVE REPEATED MY STORY A DOZEN TIMES before I was allowed to head to my room. I still hadn't eaten anything and my stomach was reminding me of that issue.

I sat on my bed and looked outside, wishing that I had a plate of eggs or some vegetables to eat.

Instead, I found I was looking at my friend Fred, standing outside my window.

He was standing behind the bushes, looking around absently. I walked to the window and tapped, getting his attention.

He waved and motioned for me to come out, and I can't tell you why, but I did.

26

Fred had been my friend for a long time. When he'd gotten aggressive in his room, I hadn't seen him like that in years. He wasn't the kind to play practical jokes, he wasn't the type of friend to make you wait or not show up when he said he would.

So, I found it odd that when I left the house, Fred wasn't outside. I made sure my parents and the other gathered adults didn't notice me when I left. I wasn't too keen on being asked a million questions again. So when I left, I kept tight to the wall and walked lightly.

I jumped down the front steps, jogged around the side of the house and stopped at the bushes outside my window.

No sign of my friend.

Now, it'd been a long few days. Heck, long doesn't do that justice. I was tired, hungry and awaiting my punishment for being a bad apple in my parents eyes. So maybe I wasn't thinking straight, but upon not seeing Fred, I shrugged my shoulders and went back inside. Most folks would've probably went and looked a bit harder, but between being foggy and hungry I thought nothing of it.

As I entered, the gathered adults were leaving and I spotted my dad's face. He didn't look all that pleased.

I waited patiently and quietly until it was just the three of us and I walked over and gave my mom a hug. While it was meant to suck up and reduce my impending sentence, I also had an inkling that even at fifteen, this was one of those moments where I needed my mom.

'Everything ok, dad?'

I felt the words spill out without thinking, and when his gaze met mine, I knew they weren't.

'They found your friend, Fred. Missing his legs. Something got him.'

My blood ran cold, my heart threatened to punch its way through my ribcage. It couldn't be.

'When?'

'While we were up at the window.'

I collapsed into my mom, I started shaking and sobbing and I couldn't breathe. My dad rushed over to help support my weight, and my parents squeezed me tight.

I managed to get the words out and when I did I saw their faces change.

'But I saw Fred, about five minutes ago, outside my window,' I said, crying even harder.

I cried until I fell asleep on my mom's shoulder.

27

When the sun hit my eyes and wrestled me from my dreams, I bolted out of bed and rushed to my window.

No sign of Fred.

I ran through the house, out the door, jumped down the steps and went around the house to the bushes below my window.

No sign of Fred.

I felt tears welling up once again. I didn't want to cry in public. Back then boys or men crying in public was shameful. If Gramps had been around he'd have helped guide me in.

But I was alone.

I started to return to the front porch when a noise caught my attention.

A clanking. The distinct sound of chains hitting each other, scuffing the ground and banging together again.

It was the same sound I'd heard that night near the window in the ground.

I should've turned and ran. Ran inside, got my dad.

Instead I went back around the house, looking for the source of the sound.

I didn't immediately notice anything, but as I kept creeping around the house I spotted my friends Judy and Liza across the street.

'What you doing?' They both hollered. I cringed at how loud they were. They weren't sisters but you wouldn't be wrong in assuming they were. Both had long brown hair, freckles on their cheeks and you never could tell which one was laughing. They liked to dress the same, and me and Fred always joked that they wished they were twins.

I jogged over, not really wanting to chat, but at the same time I didn't feel good being by myself. The window in the ground was far away, yet I was hearing the chain sounds here and seeing Fred. That wasn't a good thing, not in the least.

'Fred's dead,' I blurted out without any consideration to how these two girls would take the news. I've tried to live my life like a gentleman, opening doors, helping the elderly with groceries. This was a low moment though, if I do say so myself. Never been proud of this one.

They both simultaneously burst into tears, hugging each other tight. My eyes were red-rimmed and wet, but I held it together. No sense in me joining them in a sidewalk spectacle.

'Liza, Judy, that's not all. I saw Fred. He was supposed to have already died, but he was standing outside my window. Do you two know about the window in the ground?'

They both shook their heads, wiping their eyes clear from tears.

'Well, there's a window in the ground. It's in a

clearing up in the mountain. We're not supposed to learn about it until we turn eighteen. Gramps showed me the other day, then I showed Fred. I'm why Fred is dead.'

I stepped into their arms and embraced them as they hugged me tight.

Even as they hugged me, I knew I shouldn't have told them. But it was the window, you see? The window wanted me to tell them, to lead them. You gotta believe me.

I sobbed and kept mumbling that I killed Fred, I was responsible. They rocked me and rubbed my back, and I knew then that they truly did care for me as a friend.

We broke the embrace, I wiped my tears away, and we faced each other.

A silent agreement passed between us.

I should've ate some breakfast because the walk was going to take some time, but we began our walk towards the window in the ground.

Three friends wanting to get some answers.

28

I CAN'T TELL YOU IF MY PERCEIVED CONNECTION with the window caused time to alter, or gave the three of us the ability to walk faster than the fastest humans on earth, but suddenly there we stood at the entrance to the trail.

Maybe it's just been the passage of time, and in my old age I'm remembering things differently?

Another few minutes and the girls were reading the rules and then I told them, like Gramps told me, to re-read them. I felt foolish because I'd told Fred to read them twice so that it'd save his life, but now he was dead. I pushed that aside though, and made sure they knew them.

Once they were done we made our way deeper into the forest, higher up the mountain, feeling the full weight of our youth being pushed down, our maturation into adults propping us back up, propelling our feet to move ever forward. If not for curiosity's sake, then for our friend. Fred had been a great friend. I wished he was walking with us now, but the cards had been dealt and I didn't have any pocket aces to change his fate.

At some point, as the hill got steeper, I found we were now holding hands. I'd never held hands with a girl before, but it was nice and calming. I looked at Judy and then at Liza and found I was looking at two girls I loved like sisters in this moment.

The grief of losing Fred was making me more introspective. At least that's what I think. And I knew then that if we all made it out of here alive, well I'd protect these two for the rest of time, like they'd protect me going forward.

The hill flattened out again and there before us was the clearing.

We arrived, just the three of us, and I was surprised. I'd half expected a group of townsfolk to be already here, discussing what was to happen going ahead.

I heard the two young women suck in their breath as they spotted the mound across the open grass. It was now afternoon but the trees were tall enough to cause a shadow to fall over the window in the ground. Even from our distance we could make out a light dancing through the glass.

'What's down there?' Judy tentatively asked, as she rose onto her toes, trying to get a better look. We were too far away to see anything, but I wasn't surprised she'd tried.

'I feel odd. Like something is whispering beside me, wanting me to go to the window,' Liza said. Her voice wavered and her cheeks were flush.

'Careful you two,' I spoke up, 'we need to make sure none of us do something reckless. Keep holding hands.'

I squeezed their hands tighter to get them focused.

'I don't like this place one bit,' Judy said.

I nodded. Then I felt Liza's hand let go of mine, and she was running. She was sprinting across the clearing, her legs covering ground at an alarming speed. I took off after her, while Judy screamed at Liza to stop from behind us.

Tough times call for tough decisions, I decided and as I got closer I leaped and football tackled her, the two of us hitting the ground hard then rolling together, bodies tangled but both of us alive.

I stood, helped her up and pushed her back towards Judy.

I wanted to prevent her from feeling the draw or even looking at the mound and the window.

Once we arrived at Judy and were beyond the grass of the clearing, Liza's body visibly relaxed and the colour of her face returned.

'What was that?' She sounded dazed and not totally sure of her surroundings.

'Whatever is *below* that window did that,' I answered and with Judy's help, we guided Liza away from the window.

We needed to put some space between us and it, and now I was certain we weren't going to find any answers about Fred.

It was time to walk back home.

29

WHILE THE WALK THERE WENT BY LICKETY-SPLIT, the walk back took forever.

Liza's knee had been skinned when I tackled her and she was having trouble walking, her limp increasing as we travelled. By the time we'd made it back to the sign post she was almost in tears.

'I'll piggy-back you,' I suggested, putting my back near her and squatting down a bit.

She accepted without saying anything and with Judy's help, she hopped on.

It was just beginning to grow dark and as we arrived at the intersection near our houses, we could see our parents were gathered, their discussion growing heated and animated.

When they saw us sheepishly walking up, I'd tell you their faces changed to joy and relief, but you already knew that. Those of you still reading along with kids understand. Those who don't, that's ok, we all follow our own paths in life. Mine led me here after all.

I caught my parents up on what'd went down and

my dad's face grew stern. When I was done, they asked us to return to our houses and that we were to stay there until needed.

It was two days later before I found out we were up a creek and the paddles were gone.

30

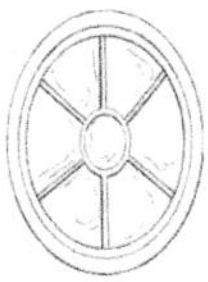

THE NEXT DAY WAS A QUIET ONE.

I woke up, ate breakfast and returned to my room. I didn't see mom or dad and just kept to myself. I read some books, played with my cars and my toy soldiers, but for the most part I found myself staring out of my window.

Maybe I was hoping Fred would be there? Who knows?

I stood and stared, I sat and watched and really all that I saw was a small snapshot of life pass before me, just outside my room.

I found myself staring *at* my window as well. Thinking about mine versus the one up there, in the mound, keeping things from our world. Odd how the mind wanders, isn't it?

I watched Judy's mom walk by on the opposite sidewalk, carrying a sack. I saw Liza's mom follow a few minutes later. At some point a bird landed on the bush and chirped and hopped. In my state of boredom I imagined that it was trying to get me to come out and play.

'Oh, no,' I said. 'Sorry, Mr. Bird, but every time I

leave the house lately I end up at that window. I need to stay put.'

Chirp, chirp, it replied, hopping and bobbing.

'Mr. Bird!' I replied in shock. I couldn't believe what he wanted me to do. I chuckled and shook my head. Nature really wanted me to misbehave.

The bird chirped again and flew away.

I made myself comfortable on the bed and drifted off.

Outside, two dozen citizens passed by on the sidewalk, holding torches.

31

THE NEXT MORNING I WOKE UP FROM THE rumbling in my stomach. I'd fallen asleep and slept straight through the night. It was unusual for me to miss any meals, especially dinner, and now in a matter of a few days I'd missed several.

I was surprised my mom wasn't checking my temperature or bringing me to Doc Williams.

A familiar clanking and clattering sound drew my attention to the window.

As I looked out at the scene before me, I had to stifle a scream.

From the number of people walking, it looked like every person who lived in town was parading down the street. They all had torches in their hands, anger in their eyes.

All accept one.

At the front of the mob was Gramps. He was naked and in shackles. His wrists and ankles were bound, a thick piece of steel connecting the metal cuffs. The chains were too long and hit the road as he shuffled along. It looked like maybe he'd put up a fight, his knees and hands were bloody, as was his face.

His head had been shaved clean of hair and looking at his downcast face, I realized his eyes were purple and swollen shut.

I heard a crack in the air and saw a man behind Gramps whip his back, causing him to howl in pain.

I rushed out of the house and ran straight into my parents, standing on the top step of our porch.

They both stood holding torches, and when they turned to look at me I fell to the ground.

Their faces were painted white with black markings.

32

VISION BLURRY.

Eyes stinging.

I was being dragged.

Clink-clink-clink.

I could hear the chains rattling on the ground. Was I chained? No. Two people had me by the armpits and I was being dragged along with the mob.

I blinked rapidly, getting my sight to clear and letting me see where we were.

I already knew in my heart, but seeing the sign post with the rules pass by sent a shiver through me.

'I'm awake,' I croaked. 'Hey? Hello? I can walk.'

The two people dragging me finally heard my pleas and stopped. I stood up and stretched. I saw with some surprise that the two people were my mom and dad.

'He brought this on himself,' my dad said. They left me standing there, walking briskly and catching up to the group.

I followed quickly after. I could have turned and ran home, but I needed to know.

I may be a coward, but my curiosity overrode my fear.

Bit of a theme now, when I think back on it.

33

We arrived at the clearing with the sun burning down on us from directly above.

The group stopped walking and began to hum lightly. The effect of one hundred or so people humming together made it sound like a hive of bees preparing to attack.

I made my way to the front of the mob and found Gramps. Even if he wanted to look me in the eyes, he couldn't. His eyes looked like two overripe plums mushed onto his face. Someone had spent some significant time punching him.

'Gramps?' I whispered, not sure if he could hear me or if he was too far gone. His head cocked up towards my voice.

'Gramps, I'm so sorry.'

He nodded and licked his blood caked lips.

'Don't worry, son. I knew what I'd done when I brought you up here.'

I hugged him, not caring that he winced in pain or that I was being covered in his sweat and blood.

Then Gramps was pulled from my arms.

The humming grew louder and from the far side of the group someone began to hit a drum.

The bom... bom... bom... of the drum created an eerie reverie. I was entranced by the sound, with the sweet scent in the air, the wind delicately filling my inhalations with summer love. All the while I watched as they led Gramps across the clearing.

As they arrived at the mound, I fell to my knees, knowing what was to come.

The group hummed louder and a large man emerged from the group and approached the window. From his height and size, I guessed it was the sheriff, but I couldn't see his face.

He grabbed a thick hook and hoisted the window open.

The warmth of the sun disappeared, as the air from below blew forth from the opening.

In one swift movement, two people pushed Gramps, a senior citizen still shackled, into the opening.

He dropped from sight and no matter how loud the group hummed and the drum bommed, I could hear Gramps being eviscerated and devoured from where I kneeled.

34

Somehow I ended up back home. I wish I could tell you how but that part of my life has been struck from the official record.

For two nights and three days I tossed and turned on my bed, the sounds of Gramps dying haunting my ears. When my eyes were closed, all I saw was that gaping window. When I opened them the shadows in my room threatened to burst forth and take me.

It was all I could do not to scream.

35

ON THE THIRD DAY MY MOTHER CAME TO CHECK on me.

She carried with her a plate of cookies and a glass of milk.

She smiled at me as she sat on the edge of my bed but I struggled to look at her.

'You ok?'

Her words startled me. I felt like it'd been years since I'd heard another human's voice.

'No,' I said and broke into heavy sobs.

'Oh, my poor boy,' she said as she cradled me in her arms and rubbed my back.

Once my crying was under control I sat up and finally looked her in the eyes. I was thankful to see my mom's face, no white makeup remaining.

'Why?'

It was all I could muster, all I could force out.

'Your grandfather knew what the town would need to do. We've had an uneasy balance with whatever that is up there. We keep it safe, it keeps us safe. We've never had an issue with food or water. It provides, we protect.'

'So... we work for that window?'

I couldn't believe this was a conversation I was having with my mom. Looking back on it now, I'm thankful she was honest and open with me. Back then, I just longed for the days of trying not to do chores.

'Kind of. It's complicated. The mayor and sheriff have agreed to not punish you or either of the girls. You've been through enough and with the loss of Fred and the sacrifice of your grandfather we should be fine for now. Your father and some men will be spending a few nights up there, just to make sure. But otherwise, consider life back to normal.'

She got up and left me. Left me with my thoughts and so many unanswered questions.

36

DID LIFE RETURN TO NORMAL?

No, it never has.

37

The first day my dad was at the window in the ground, I laid low.

This was becoming a common cycle for me. Do something I shouldn't, then try and be invisible. It seems to be a common cycle for most kids at that age.

I read, swept the floors and did some wash.

When I hung the clothes on the dry line outside, I smiled at the feeling of the sun's rays on my face, the warmth beating back some of the blackness that had begun to worm its way into my ribcage.

Once that was done, I grabbed a blanket from the hall closet and laid it on some grass in the front yard by the big tree and leaned up against it.

It just felt good to be outside, but in the relative safety of the front of the house. I didn't think I could stomach doing this at any picnic spots and definitely not in any of the places Fred and I used to frequent in the woods.

I waved at some of the neighbors as they walked by. Odd how random strangers' lives can be intersected for one singular second. In that brief encounter we smile, nod, maybe wink, and then move on.

Within an hour it's forgotten, but for a moment the universe put us together in the same place at the same time.

I sat under the sun as it grew sleepy, dipping its head under the covers for the night.

The moon began to ascend above. I thought about if man would ever step foot on that big piece of rock so far away.

My mom came out with my dinner on a plate. She sat beside me on the blanket quietly while I ate. When I was done, I asked if dad would be coming home that night.

She took her time before standing and replying.

'I'm not sure he'll ever come home, honey,' she said, before heading into the house.

38

After my mom's cryptic reply I found my mind was racing.

Why wouldn't dad come back? What was actually happening up there? Were more people being tossed into the open window? Was my dad being punished instead of me?

I waited before returning into the house, entering to the sound of my mom gently snoring.

I wanted to wake her up and demand that we go see dad. I wanted to shout and scream and throw a glass of water against the wall, like they did in all the books I read. Really let the world know I was pissed and demanded action.

Instead, I walked to my room, closed the door and tried to sleep.

A coward needs to make his bed and lie in it.

Now that may make you angry, and believe me, it made me angry too. But what was I going to do? I was a fifteen year old kid who'd been shown the town secret and caused the death of his gramps. Oh, yes and my friend, Fred. Almost forgot about him.

I had no leg to stand on.

But, as I said earlier, at some point during that walk with gramps to the window in the ground, I'd went from being a kid to an adult. Now I needed to make an adult decision.

I got up, left my room and shook my mom awake.

She rubbed her eyes and looked at me confused.

'Take me to see dad,' I said, and left her room before she could say no.

I waited outside with my jacket on. I felt sure she wouldn't come.

I heard the door open and there she stood.

Then we walked.

39

UNDER THE EVER WATCHING LIGHT OF THE MOON, I held my mom's hand and walked beside her.

We soon left those rules on the sign post behind us, rules that by now had etched themselves into the folds of my brain.

I was already taller than her, but from behind, the shadows showed an outline of a mom holding the hand of her toddler. It was fitting, truly.

I'd never felt smaller, never felt meeker. What if we were too late?

I reminisced about all of the great memories I had with my dad. I'd never see Gramps alive again, but the thought of losing my dad made my stomach contents flop and my eyes burn.

It wasn't until we'd conquered the hill and reached the flat path before the clearing that the noises from ahead of us began to cut through the night's splendor.

You ever been to a pig slaughter?

Pigs are precious creatures, but most folks will tell you they're also some of the most delicious animals on the planet.

Every year we'd raise one or two pigs, usually penning them up at Gramps'. I'd help feed them sometimes, but Gramps always warned me to stay back.

'You fall in,' he'd say, 'they'll eat you up before you know what's happened.'

The day of the year I hated the most was slaughtering day. My dad would get my butt out of bed bright and early. We'd drive to Gramps and walk to the pen. Then the carnage would begin.

I ask if you've been to a pig slaughtering for one reason and one reason only.

The screams.

When pigs are being killed they scream just like a human. Horrible, ear shattering screams that make you weak in the knees and instantly regret taking part in this process.

Those were the same sounds we heard as we approached the clearing.

My mom stopped walking and craned her neck to see if she could spot what was going to greet us, but she just wasn't tall enough.

'You stay here, ok honey? I'll check what's going on.'

Before I could reply she was gone, leaving me alone in the scariest place on the face of the planet.

I know now scarier places exist. Hell, some are just below our feet. But standing there, all by my fraidy-cat self. I wished I was invisible.

I was still frozen in place when my mom came rushing back. Her face showed fear beyond anything my young brain could comprehend.

'What is it, mom?'

She looked at me, looked back towards the mound, then me again.

She was breathing rapidly and I could see sweat on her forehead.

'They've... they've... captured something from below,' she exclaimed.

Somehow my eyes stayed in my head.

My mom grabbed me moments before I took off running into the clearing.

'I don't think you should go,' she said. She was looking me directly in my eyes, trying to get me to focus on her.

Then an extremely violent roar boomed from the direction of the window and we heard men yelling and more of the pigs-being-slaughtered screams.

'Mom? Mommy?'

I started to panic. Should we run? Should we hide? I didn't know what to do.

How was I to know what to do? Think on that for five fucking seconds! I know you're sitting there, staring at this before you, judging me. You weren't there, you weren't there. God. The sounds. Why did Gramps do this to me? WHY?

She pulled me by my arm, harder than she intended I think, but it felt like my arm was going to snap off. We rushed off the path and hid where me and Fred had been hiding when we saw the chain-parade before.

Men rushed by and in a blur my mom lunged out and grabbed someone, pulling them into the underbrush. I jumped into my dad's outstretched arms when I saw it was him. In that moment, with my mom and dad hugging me, I realized I truly did believe I'd never expected to see him alive again.

40

WELL FRIENDS, WE'RE GETTING CLOSER TO THE end here. Life has a way of sneaking up on you, kicking you when you're down.

I wish this had a happy ending. In some ways, I guess it does. If you've read this far, I'd think you're at least smarter than me.

Or maybe that says the opposite? Maybe you're just like me. Curious. If you stumble on a window in the ground in the woods, would you want to go look? Bet so.

Bet so.

We stayed huddled under those branches for hours. When you're scared and certain you're going to die, minutes feel like hours, hours like days. My knees ached, my ankles cried out in agony and I just wanted to be home and in my bed.

All around us we could hear the butchery. Howls, screeches and snarls carried across the night air, punctuated by the slapping noises of meat hitting rocks and bones being snapped.

I kept my eyes shut tight and at some point I'd covered my ears with my hands. My mom and dad kept me wrapped in their arms and even between them I didn't feel safe.

With my eyes and ears covered I could still hear how close those *things* from below were, I could feel the ground vibrate and bounce under their massive weight. At one point I'm even certain something immense flew across the sky, its wings blocking out the light from the moon.

As the vicious battle escalated beyond our hiding spot I felt my parent's body positions shift. It was no longer protective but submissive. They'd resigned to our fate.

It was the end.

But then we heard a voice. A man yelling my parents' names. Suddenly, we were moving.

I opened my eyes and saw blood and body parts everywhere. We hustled across the path and were pulled into a hollowed out base of a tree. The sheriff was there, as were four other adults I recognized but whose names I didn't know.

Nobody spoke. Nobody made eye contact.

We all huddled together quietly, patiently, waiting until the dying were dead.

41

THE GURGLES AND MOANS STOPPED JUST BEFORE dawn.

I'd fallen asleep standing up, leaning against my mom.

I shuddered awake at the sound of a loud bang echoing and I knew immediately that the window in the ground had been slammed shut.

'This was all because of me, wasn't it?'

My small voice caused the group to jump, one person clutching their chest as though they were going to pass out.

'Your grandpa shouldn't have brought you here,' the sheriff replied angrily. 'You're connected in some way. Why? How? We don't know. But those *things* below, they want you.'

The sheriff's words cut through my bravado. I was just a kid. A kid! I hadn't had a girlfriend, no first kiss.

I was supposed to grow up, move away, enjoy the big city life before returning home and settling down. I'd fall in love with Judy or Liza, or if they'd already married it would be someone else and we'd have a few kids. We'd get a dog and on Sunday's we'd attend church. All the time I'd never once think about the pathway, the rules, the clearing, or the godforsaken window in the ground.

I looked at my mom. Then my dad. This was all because I'd upset the order of things. Sure, Gramps had shown me the window when he shouldn't have, but I was the one who couldn't stay away. Now, whatever compelled me to keep coming back was growing stronger and pulling harder.

'Then they can have me,' I said, trying to muster a triumphant tone.

'No!' My mother screamed in horror at what I said, my dad grabbed her and pulled her close, catching her before she hit the ground. I saw she was barely holding on to consciousness.

'Mom, it's the only way,' I said, before they both wrapped me in a hug. We were all sobbing, my parents devastation bared before the others. As I stood and turned to face my decision, the realization of what I was willing to do weighed my feet down.

As I marched out of the tree hollow and maneuvered through the corpses littering the clearing, I walked towards that mound with a sense of purpose.

I heard the survivors moving behind me. Was that my mom I could still hear crying? I hoped not. I hoped so.

When I arrived at the base of the mound, I could feel a disturbance from below, and the shadows I could make out within the window looked like a swarm of sharks attacking a bloody bucket of chum. They danced and darted around, the light creating a rhythmic motion.

The sheriff walked over and picked up the massive steel hook and before I could protest he affixed it to the frame of the window and hoisted it open.

The stench that emitted from within caused half of the people still alive to vomit.

My mom was on me, holding me tight, squeezing me as only a mother can.

I felt my dad's hand on my shoulder and then his scratchy whiskers against my face as he kissed me on the cheek.

'I'll miss you,' I said, as they stepped back.

I looked at the alive. I knew this was my fate.

I turned and jumped through the opening, the window clattering shut behind me.

42

So HERE WE ARE.

You're all caught up.

Well, almost.

You see, that all happened close to two hundred years ago.

I landed on the hard dirt floor and the *things* below jumped out of the light.

I said 'here I am, do what you will.' They've mostly left me alone ever since.

Many times over the years I swore I could hear crying from above. Was it my mother? At first, probably. After. My memories.

I'm the guardian of the light.

I keep the single candle burning. If you come at night and see a glow from below, that's my candle.

But time is running short.

I've been sitting on this wooden rocking chair, looking out a window at the sky above for two centuries.

Now, I've felt a change creeping into me for the last fifty or so years. My feet are growing longer, wider and my back aches. Pretty sure I'm sprouting wings. I can't reach back and feel 'em, but when I sit in this chair I have to sit just right so those knobs don't ache against the wood.

I never saw my mom or dad again. Two decades after I sacrificed myself, Judy was tossed down. She screamed and begged for her life, but the creatures weren't ready for someone to take my place yet. They devoured her before I even got a word out.

The pattern repeats. Every so often a new person is tossed in for whatever reason, but I'm still here, still enough human left to keep my job.

During the day, I melt down the material that the creatures bring at night, making more candles.

At night I wrap the leather straps around my ankles and waist, making sure nothing will take me while I sleep. I've been stirred from my sleep before by a creature getting too close. Had a few scratches as well, little reminders that it's a tentative respect between me and them. Not sure why, but down here I don't need to eat or drink nothing. Good thing, as there's no food anywhere.

What's my purpose? Making the candles? Good question.

I think they need a light.

Why?

Personally, I think there's something even worse deeper below. The creatures need the light to keep them safe, somewhere far from *whatever* it is they're scared of. Sounds silly, sure. But aren't we all a little scared of the dark?

As this change takes hold, I felt it best to finally make the effort to write down my story. Hope I don't sound too crazy. I haven't spoken to another person since that night. Not even sure I *could* speak at this point.

As I end this tale and get ready to join the rest of these abominations below, I just hope they choose an older person next time. I missed out on my life and I still shed tears over the joys I never experienced. Oh well, no need to kick that dead dog again, right?

I'm introspective enough to know that sometimes life above that window has been just as bad to some as this old timer below.

Hell, from some of the newsprint those winged things have scavenged, I'm kind of glad I've missed most of what humans have endured.

If it's you that comes down that hole, I'm so sorry.

I can't promise you'll be taking my job. You may very well just be another sacrifice for the things.

But if it is you that ends up down here, relieving me of my position, I'm still sorry.

You'd have been better off if you'd never found out about the window in the ground.

AFTERWORD

Hey friends. Welcome back!

Hope you enjoyed what the hell you just read. I know I had a lot of fun writing it.

This was one of those stories that came to me from a random moment. My wife, my son and I were enjoying a walk at a small nature sanctuary near us, twenty minute drive away. It's called the Clifford E. Lee Nature Sanctuary and we love going and walking there. We went one year, spring time, still snow on the ground. On one of the loops, my son ran ahead and while we were catching up, we came up a small hill and off in the distance I noticed one area of grass that was completely clear of snow. It was bright green, as though someone had been maintaining it. I snapped a picture – even sent it to David Sodergren at one point. Later on, me and my son were playing in his sand table and I covered a plastic toy with sand, exposing the window. It clicked. It was a moment where most of the story just plopped into my massive head. Eureka!

AFTERWORD

Big thanks to the beta readers on this one. This story is similar for myself as Ritual was, in that I wrote it and then wasn't wholly sure on what the hell I just put onto paper and it was the beta readers (as always) that said I was on to something. I do want to mention – Jim from One Legged Reviews had made a suggestion, and this was one of the few times I completely decided to not work on that idea. He suggested I add more back story, more info on how the window got there etc. I liked the idea, but the more I tried to work on it, the harder I found a spot to put it but also how to make it flow in this 'journal' style of a read. So, my apologies Jim!

As you may have noticed, this release came out through the new-ish The Writing Collective. This is an upstart micro-publisher (not even sure if that's accurate!) that a few amazing folks have started up. I connected with them when I was asked to write the foreword for their anthology 'Lost Voices.' If you haven't checked that out, you really should. They've already released a number of amazing books and I'm pretty excited and humbled that they've decided to add this book to their roster. So, thanks TWC!

Thanks to Mason for the rad cover, David for input and edits and all the beta-readers who gave me feedback. Some of them read draft one, some draft two and some draft three, so it was unique to see how things worked or didn't over the few months this was out with them!

Lastly, thanks to everyone else out there. Seriously. My friends, family, authors, bloggers etc. Everyone who I interact with on a daily, weekly or monthly basis. I've always said I purely write for me and to read the type of book I would want to read. To see even one other person say – 'I can't wait to see what you come up with next!' is mind blowing and so amazing.

So cheers!

Until we meet again. And if you know my output – it'll probably be sooner than later!

Steve

ABOUT THE AUTHOR

Steve Stred writes dark, bleak horror fiction.

Steve is the author of three novels, a number of novellas and four collections.

He is proud to work with the Ladies of Horror Fiction to facilitate the Annual LOHF Writers Grant.

Steve is also a voracious reader, reviewing everything he reads and submitting the majority of his reviews to be featured on Kendall Reviews.

Steve Stred is based in Edmonton, AB, Canada and lives with his wife, his son and their dog OJ.

Website: stevestredauthor.wordpress.com
Twitter @stevestred
Instagram @stevestred

ALSO BY STEVE STRED

Novels

- Invisible

- The Stranger

- Piece of Me

- The Boy Whose Room Was Outside

Novellas

- YURI

- Jane: the 816 Chronicles

- Wagon Buddy

- The Girl Who Hid in the Trees

- The One That Knows No Fear

- Ritual

Collections

- Frostbitten: 12 Hymns of Misery

- Left Hand Path: 13 more tales of black magick

- Dim the Sun

- The Night Crawls In

ABOUT THE PUBLISHER

The Writing Collective (TWC) is a band of writers who have a passion for writing and getting fabulous works of fiction into the hands of readers.

We have an author centric approach to publishing and work hard at providing authors a platform for their works and a publishing model that ensures that they get paid for what they write.

Here at the TWC we are continually reading and discovering new and talented writers who deserve that little push into the publishing world and with our unique model and collected experiences we hope to help get your book out into the world and into the hands of readers.

Save Game a novel by *Joseph Sale*

Available from Amazon.

Lost Voices is a collection of short fiction by *Joseph Sale, Emily Harrison, Christa Wojciechowski and Ross Jeffery.*

Available from Amazon.

Juniper is the debut novella by *Ross Jeffery*

Available from Amazon

The Fabric of Tombstones is the debut flash fiction collection from *B.F. Jones*

Available from Amazon

Printed in Great Britain
by Amazon

34064679R00066